DISCARD

Volcanoes

Catherine Chambers

Heinemann Library
Chicago, Illinois

© 2001 Reed Educational & Professional Publishing
Published by Heinemann Library,
an imprint of Reed Educational & Professional Publishing,
100 N. LaSalle, Suite 1010
Chicago, IL 60602
Customer Service 888-454-2279
Visit our website at www.heinemannlibrary.com

Designed by Celia Floyd
Originated by Dot Gradations
Printed by Wing King Tong in Hong Kong

05 04 03 02 01
10 9 8 7 6 5 4 3 2 1

Library of Congress Cataloging-in-Publication Data

Chambers, Catherine, 1954-
    Volcanoes / Catherine Chambers.
       p. cm. — (Disasters in nature)
    Includes bibliographical references and index.
    Summary: Examines the formation and eruption of volcanoes and describes the damages that they can cause.
    ISBN 1-57572-431-6 (lib. bdg.)
    1. Volcanoes—Juvenile literature. [1. Volcanoes.] I. Title.

QE521.3.C46 2000
551.21—dc21   99-462206

Acknowledgments

The Publishers would like to thank the following for permission to reproduce photographs:

Planet Earth Pictures/Krafft, pp. 5, 17, 39; Planet Earth Pictures/Durieux, p. 6; Panos/Rob Huibers, pp. 7, 9, 34; FLPA/USDA Forest Service, p. 11; Katz Pictures/Donatello Brogioni, p. 11; FLPA/S. Jonasson, pp. 16, 33; BBC Natural History Unit/Michael Pitts, p. 20; Planet Earth Pictures/John Lythgoe, p. 21; Corbis/Peter Turnley, p. 22; Panos/Chris Stowers, p. 23; FLPA/M. Zhilin, p. 24; Bruce Coleman Collection/Charlie Ott, p. 25; Oxford Scientific Films/Dieter & Mary Plage, p. 27; Planet Earth Pictures/Bourseiller & Durieux, pp. 29, 42; Environmental Images/Phil Harris, p. 31; FLPA/Panda/G. Tomarchio, p. 32; Photri, p. 35; Corbis, p. 37; Dennis Flaherty, p. 37; BBC Natural History Unit/Georgette Douwman, p. 41; Pictor, p. 43; Planet Earth Pictures/Richard Coomber, p. 45.

Cover photograph reproduced with permission of Still Pictures.

Our thanks to Matthew Slagel of the University of Chicago for his comments in the preparation of this book.

Every effort has been made to contact copyright holders of any material reproduced in this book. Any omissions will be rectified in subsequent printings if notice is given to the Publisher.

Some words are shown in bold, **like this.** You can find out what they mean by looking in the glossary.

Contents

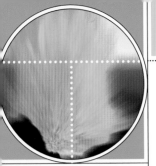

What Is a Volcano?

A volcano is an eruption of ash, gases, and molten rock from below the earth's crust. The deadly substances spurt or ooze through cracks and faults, up into the sky and over the land. As they cool, the **lava** and ash form new landscapes. A volcanic cone forms above the ground, with a deep, empty **crater** at the center where lava, gas, and ash once pushed through. However, none of these amazing volcanic features occur without some destruction of the natural world around them. Frequently there is loss of human life. A huge volcanic eruption is nearly always a natural disaster.

Volcanoes are a devastating form of natural disaster. This is an eruption of a volcano on the island of Reunion in the Indian Ocean.

Where do volcanoes happen?

Extinct volcanoes can be found all over the world, their shapes worn down over time. Most active volcanoes have formed where the earth's crust is fractured. These breaks are marked by massive ridges and troughs that cut across ocean beds and dry land. The map on page 5 shows where they are. The fractures are moving all the time, causing pressure on sticky, molten rock lying beneath the earth's surface. When this rock gets hot enough, it becomes **buoyant,** and a volcano erupts when it rises to the surface.

Volcanoes in our hands

Some volcanoes appear to be dead and some seem to be **dormant.** Even those that are considered to be active can stay quiet for decades. All these volcanoes concern the people living near them, but no one, not even **vulcanologists,** can be certain that a volcano is safe. Some erupt after lying dormant for thousands of years. This makes it very difficult to predict volcanic eruptions. However, archaeological evidence and remains are preserved in the hot lava flow and ash. This has helped scientists not only to predict what might happen to those volcanoes in future eruptions, but also to paint an accurate picture of life long ago in areas close to volcanoes.

Volcanoes on our minds

With global satellite communications we can follow the story of an active volcano as it unfolds—from the first puffs of smoke to the final burst of gas, ash, and lava. Long ago, people had no way of knowing about volcanoes erupting far away, but eyewitness accounts show that people living nearby observed volcanic eruptions very closely.

This map shows where most of the world's active volcanoes are. Many of them lie along **tectonic plate boundaries.**

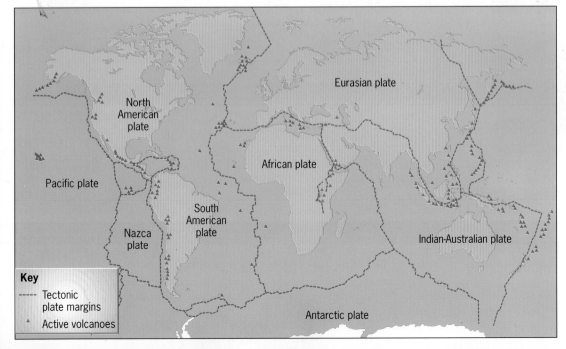

Eurasian plate

North American plate

Pacific plate

African plate

Nazca plate

South American plate

Indian-Australian plate

Key

----- Tectonic plate margins

▲ Active volcanoes

Antarctic plate

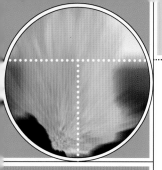

Montserrat

Montserrat, a British territory in the Caribbean, is often called the Emerald Isle. It was once a small, thriving island, but it now lies deserted. Its capital city has disappeared, and much of the once lush vegetation is covered in ash.

The giant wakes

Montserrat's volcanic Soufriere Hills had been **dormant** for 100 years, but in July 1995 steam and gas emerged from small, high **vents**—one of the first signs of volcanic activity. Within a few days, small explosions began and scientists warned that "the big one" would erupt soon. People prepared for the worst. Farmers began to harvest their crops quickly and moved their animals to safety. As a heavy shower of ash covered the capital, Plymouth, the citizens were advised to **evacuate.**

Many of the island's 11,000 people, who occupied the southern half, moved to the north. They waited for the worst to pass, but it didn't. The whole south of the island turned gray as ash smothered everything in sight. Montserrat's economy, based on agriculture, was ruined. Over half the population left the island altogether.

As the volcano on Monserrat continued rumbling and erupting, a new delta of land was built out into the sea from lava and ash flows.

A year after the volcano awoke, it still showed no sign of going back to sleep. Its top swelled into two **domes** that eventually collapsed. A **lava** flow swept down the steep valleys and into the ocean, and a new **delta** of land was created. By December 2, 1996, **vulcanologists** predicted that the volcano would throw out 387 million tons of ash and rock. It had already erupted 66 million tons in the week before the prediction. The British **Geological** Survey team and a top U.S. vulcanologist watched the situation closely.

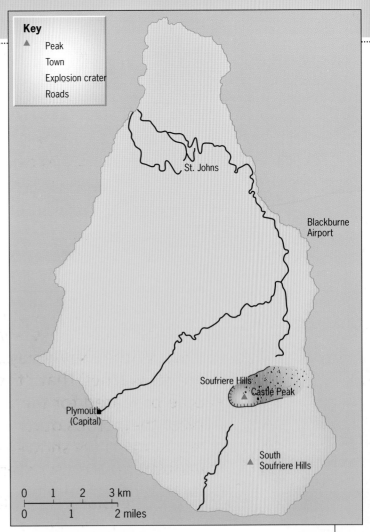

Montserrat's volcanoes are in the southeast.

The giant roars

In May 1997, superheated ash, rock, and gas were thrown thousands of feet into the air, and the alert level was raised from amber to orange—just two colors away from the highest warning. The Montserrat Volcano Observatory warned that more people would have to evacuate the island, especially the 120 who remained in high-risk areas in the center and south.

In June, bigger eruptions rocked the island. On June 25, **pyroclastic flows** ran down the volcano's sides at over 125 miles (200 kilometers) per hour, smothering entire villages. Twenty people were killed—the first casualties recorded. The south finally became totally uninhabitable, and everyone left the island. In August, more eruptions gushed from the Soufriere Hills, and they have been spitting and oozing ever since.

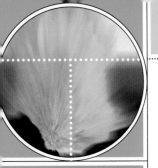

After the Disaster

What have we learned?

Scientists learned a lot about the formation of volcanoes as they watched the first of two new volcanic **domes** grow. It began in September 1995 as a small tube of sticky **magma** rising inside the **crater.** This type of molten rock is called **andesitic lava** when it erupts. It is thick and oozes out slowly, cooling into a lump. As more lava appears and oozes over the top, layers cover the lump and harden until it grows into a dome.

As it grows, the dome keeps more lava from coming out of the crater. New magma presses against the old volcano walls as it expands. This is exactly what happened in Montserrat. The dome became more and more dangerous as it grew until, in September 1996, the pressure forced landslides of hard lava and rock from the old volcano walls. This pressure also caused the violent **pyroclastic flows** of June 1997. Quite simply, the dome exploded. Then it grew again, and exploded again—a continually repeating pattern that is characteristic of these volcanic domes.

By August 1997, two-thirds of Monserrat's 40 square miles (104 square kilometers) were left completely uninhabitable. Lava flows, ash, and volcanic **pumice** stone smothered the natural vegetation and swamped the towns.

Soufriere means "sulfurous," and sulfur-bearing compounds form a large part of the gas that rises from active volcanoes. The Soufriere Hills on Montserrat are a cluster of volcanic domes, some of which formed over three million years ago. The new dome formed by the recent eruptions now rises more than 660 feet (200 meters) from the ground, and over 3,300 feet (1,000 meters) above sea level.

The political fallout

Natural disasters often reveal the political problems of a country, which may have been simmering deep under the surface for a long time. The problems caused by the eruption on Montserrat led to the resignation of the island's chief minister. There was criticism of him and the British government for not offering enough compensation to people who had to flee their homes. But the residents of Montserrat also used the disaster to make a case for being granted full British citizenship, which they had never had.

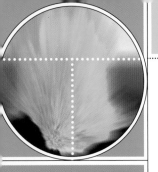

Hitting the Headlines

When the first wisps of smoke spiraled into the air on Montserrat, newspapers and television networks throughout the Caribbean realized what it could lead to. Nearby, the United States also took great interest in developments, and there was detailed coverage on the major television networks and on CNN.

However, even though Montserrat is a territory of the United Kingdom, there was little media coverage there until the first explosions led to the **evacuation** of the island. Mainland Britain has no experience of volcano disaster, and it was difficult for the media and the nation to understand the scale of the problem.

Volcano notes

Satellite communications and the Internet have made news instantly available. This is a quote from the governor of Montserrat, when the capital city was hit by an eruption. His words were quickly broadcast around the world:

"It's a huge fan-shape of destruction. Most buildings are either burned out or covered in debris. Ash deposits are up to four feet thick...We haven't used the city for so long now..."

Powerful nations

Volcanic activity in the United States, Japan, and Italy gets extensive news coverage. It also arouses a lot of media interest from the rest of the world. This is partly because these powerful nations are carefully watched, and many reporters are sent to cover their stories.

These countries have spent millions of dollars on trying to predict volcanoes and creating warning systems. They also have trained many **vulcanologists.** This means that there is a huge wealth of scientific information and knowledge for the rest of the world to share.

In times of trouble, other nations call upon the aid of vulcanologists from the United States, Japan, and Italy. This helps to draw media interest from other parts of the world and raise awareness of what small islands like Montserrat face.

A photographer stayed around long enough to record the avalanche of debris and then the huge eruption that removed a big chunk of Mount St. Helens, in Washington state, in 1980. The pictures he took help us to understand how eruptions occur.

Although news coverage tends to concentrate on sensational stories, it does put volcanoes in the spotlight. This encourages the study of volcanoes and ways of preventing human death and destruction.

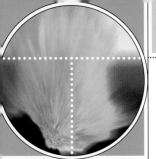

Where and How?

There are about 15,000 active volcanoes throughout the world. They occur on all continents except Australia. The greatest numbers are found in the Pacific Ring of Fire, a chain of volcanoes surrounding the Pacific Basin. It includes Japan, Indonesia, and the Philippines. Some of these lie quietly, ready to explode at any moment, while others hiss and spit all the time. Most volcanoes can be found near deep trenches in the earth's crust.

Beneath the earth's crust lies the **mantle,** a layer of hot rock about as stiff as modeling clay. Beneath the mantle lies the hot core at the center of the earth. It is thought that the high temperatures at the earth's core heat up portions of the mantle. The soft rock swells and rises as it is heated. When it presses against the cold crust, it cools, shrinks, and sinks again. Scientists believe that the continual rise and fall of the mantle is what breaks the more rigid crust into great expanses known as **tectonic plates.** These huge plates collide into each other or pull apart from each other as they are moved by the mantle.

The volcano rises

Volcanoes are formed as the result of **magma** rising through the earth's crust. Many of them involve activity along the edges of tectonic plates. So far, scientists have defined three main ways in which volcanoes are formed.

1. Sometimes the edges of tectonic plates push together. When this happens, the denser crust sinks below the less dense crust. The sinking crust gets hotter, and this causes melting. Hot magma forms in the upper part of the mantle and rises up against the crust, eventually erupting into volcanoes. The areas where this type of volcanic formation occurs are called **subduction zones.**

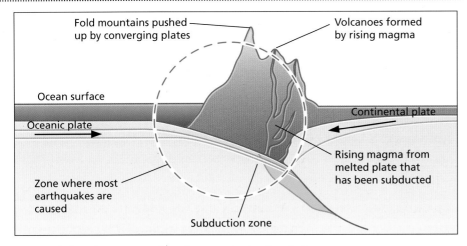

Fold mountains pushed up by converging plates

Volcanoes formed by rising magma

Ocean surface

Continental plate

Oceanic plate

Rising magma from melted plate that has been subducted

Zone where most earthquakes are caused

Subduction zone

In a subduction zone, the denser tectonic plate sinks beneath the less dense plate. Volcanoes form directly above the point where the subducted plate is melted and becomes magma.

2. Most volcanoes occur under the sea—only the largest rise above the surface to form islands. These volcanoes form at places where tectonic plates pull apart, allowing magma to rise up between them. This not only causes eruptions but also creates new crust along the edges of the plates, especially where they spread apart. The movement of these cracks is called **sea-floor spreading.**

3. Volcanoes can also occur well away from the edges of tectonic plates, right in the middle of the plates themselves. They form over **hotspots**—areas where heat rises straight from the earth's core, making magma rise through the crust, forming very large volcanic cones.

While most volcanoes are formed by similar processes, their shape and structure can vary, depending on their magma type and rate of eruption.

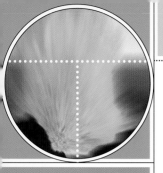

Inside a Volcano

The earth is far too deep and hot for **vulcanologists** to explore completely. The knowledge we have has been gained by studying volcanic rocks and features on the earth's surface, looking at the sun, and studying other planets.

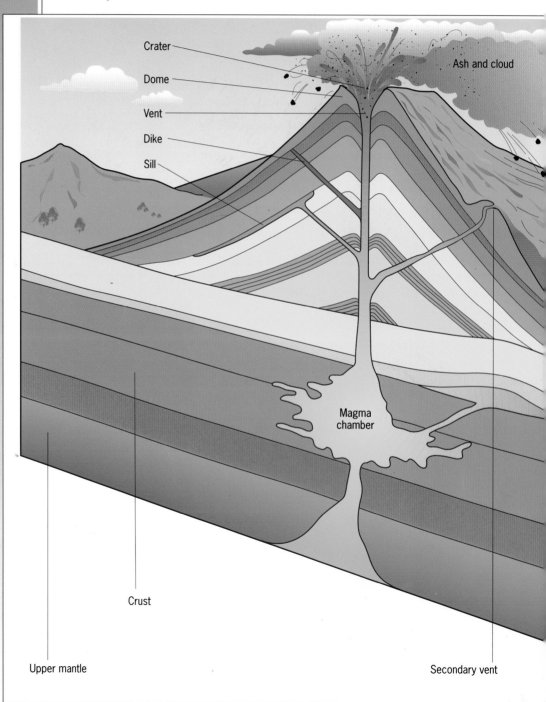

Crater

Dome

Vent

Dike

Sill

Ash and cloud

Magma chamber

Crust

Upper mantle

Secondary vent

This diagram shows several types of volcanic landscape. In real life, these would not all be found together, but several formations can occur within the same area, or quite close to one another. We will discover more about each of these features on the following pages.

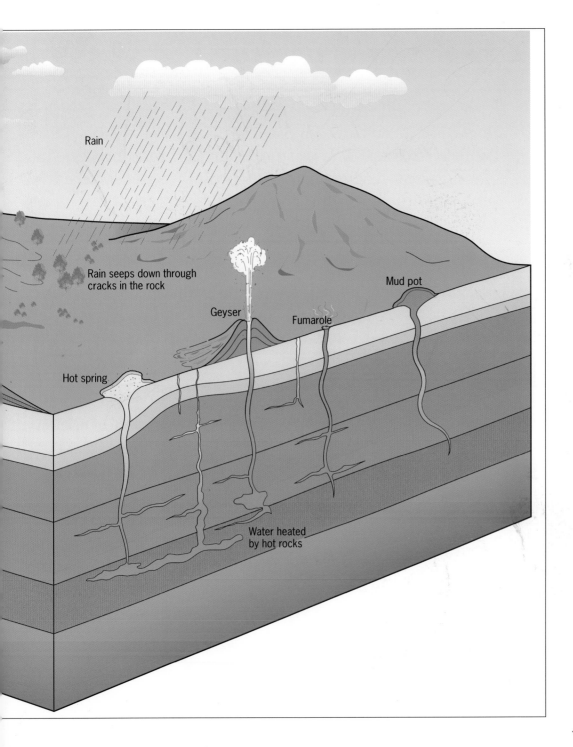

Rain

Rain seeps down through cracks in the rock

Geyser

Fumarole

Mud pot

Hot spring

Water heated by hot rocks

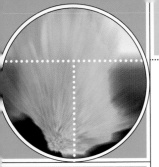

Making Volcano Shapes

When **vulcanologists** look at a volcanic landscape, they can tell the types of eruption that have occurred, and the kinds of rock that make the shapes they can see. They also have a good idea of how a future explosion would take place and the kind of damage it might do.

Explosive ingredients

As **lava** explodes into the air or creeps along the ground, it reforms into different types of rock, creating a variety of volcanic landscapes. The three main types of rock formed by lava are explained in the box on the facing page. They can vary according to the different ingredients within the lava, the type of eruption, its strength, and how long it lasts. Continual eruptions will regularly add material to a volcano, building up its shape. Rare eruptions will leave the volcano resting, but its shape will change over time as rain and wind **erode** it. Sometimes, a volcanic landscape will include more than one type of volcano.

In 1973, on the island of Heimeay in Iceland, thick, slow-moving lava smothered part of the town of Vestmannaeyjar. Then it flowed into the sea, creating new land.

Solidified lava is made up of different kinds of silicate **minerals.** These are a combination of **silicon,** oxygen, and other elements. There are three main types of lava. Each erupts in a different way and gives different shapes to the landscape. The more **silica** the lava contains, the thicker and stickier, or **viscous,** it is. When it erupts, it explodes with great force because gas has a harder time escaping. Runnier lavas flow faster and spread out more thinly.

Volcano notes

- **Basalt** is formed from a very runny lava that erupts often but gently. It contains less than 55 percent silica. When basaltic lava hardens, it forms **cinder cones** and **shield volcanoes.**

- **Andesite** is formed from steadily-flowing lava of medium viscosity that contains 55–70 percent silica. Layers of hardened andesitic lava and ash form **composite volcanoes.** These are usually very regular in shape, with slopes of about 45°.

- **Rhyolite** is formed from very thick, viscous lava that contains over 70 percent silica. Rhyolitic lava flows quite slowly and builds up into steep-sided domes. Rhyolitic magma can also form **calderas.**

The directions taken by the lava flows are often impossible to predict. Some are very disruptive, such as this one, which has completely blocked a road in Hawaii.

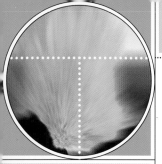

Erratic Eruptions

The shape of a volcanic landscape depends on the type of eruption that takes place, and on how long it lasts—anywhere from a few hours to several years!

Strombolian eruptions throw out **basaltic** and **andesitic** cinder and **lava** bombs in tall, sparkling fountains. The cascading and solidifying lava piles up around the vent, forming **cinder cones.**

Plinian eruptions shoot funnels of hot ash and gases high up into the air. The ash and gases can reach about 30 miles (50 kilometers) into the sky and can get blown all the way around the world.

Hawaiian eruptions are relatively mild. They spew gas and sprays of red-hot lava out of long cracks and **vents** in the ground. When the lava falls back to earth, it forms fast-flowing streams that run down the sides of the volcano. These streams can pool to form lava lakes.

Icelandic eruptions are quite calm. Lava oozes gently out of long, deep cracks in the surface.

Vesuvian eruptions are massive explosions, often from volcanoes that have been quiet for hundreds of years. **Magma** and gas build up behind a hardened lava plug and erupt violently into the air, forming billowing clouds that shower ash far and wide.

Under the earth

We cannot see all stages of a volcanic eruption because not all of it is occurs above the earth's surface. Some activity occurs quietly and slowly beneath layers of rock. Magma seeps upwards into the earth's crust and eventually solidifies. It is only revealed when the overlying layers have been **eroded** by wind and rain. The diagrams on the facing page show some of the features that underground volcanic activity can create.

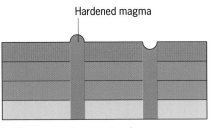

Hardened magma

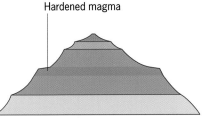

Hardened magma

Dikes are formed when magma forces its way up through vertical cracks in layers of rock. As the magma solidifies, it leaves a thin sheet or wall of rock, parting the layers like a wedge.

Sills are created by magma forcing its way between horizontal layers of rock. As the magma solidifies, it makes its own layer.

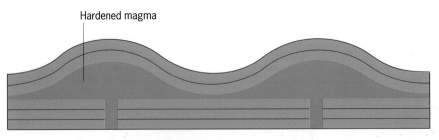

Hardened magma

Laccoliths form as magma works its way between layers of rock. It then swells, pushing the upper layer into a mound.

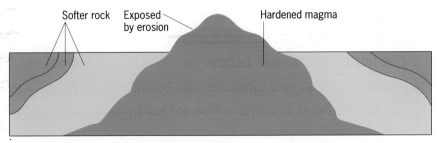

Hardened magma

Phacoliths are similar to sills, except here the magma has forced its way into layers of folded rock.

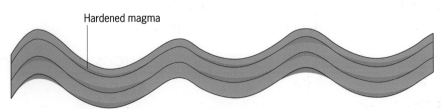

Softer rock Exposed by erosion Hardened magma

Batholiths are similar to laccoliths, but instead of just pushing the upper layer up, they displace the surrounding rock. When the layers above the batholith are eroded, the batholith itself sticks out. This is because it has hardened into very strong **granite** that erodes more slowly than the softer layers of rock above it.

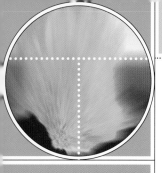

Lava Land

Volcanoes make a range of shapes in the landscape.

Dome volcanoes are formed mainly from very **viscous rhyolitic** magma. The sticky magma oozes up slowly and piles into a dome shape, often underneath a layer of hard rock. Domes can form on the side of existing volcanoes, like the one that eventually split open on the side of Mount St. Helens. A dome can also form when thick magma extrudes onto the surface, forming a round hill shape.

Calderas are huge **craters** that can be nearly 40 miles (60 kilometers) in diameter. They occur when large blocks of crust overlying a huge **magma chamber** collapse into the chamber. The magma then erupts violently around the blocks, showering ash and rock over a large area and leaving a huge hole.

Volcanoes come in a range of formations, depending on the type of lava erupting from them. Composite volcanoes, like this volcano on Komodo Island, Indonesia, are often very regular in shape.

Volcano notes

- Acids and other chemicals found in magma include fluorine, hydrochloric acid, hydrofluoric acid, sulfur dioxide, and sulfuric acid.

- Gases found in magma include ammonia, carbon dioxide, and carbon monoxide. Hydrochloric acid, hydrofluoric acid, sulfur dioxide, and sulfuric acid are also present in gas form.

- Problems humans and animals face when they breathe in gases and acids include **suffocation,** blood poisoning, burns inside and outside the body, lung infections, and irritation of the eyes, skin, nose, and throat.

Glowing and flowing

In a **Plinian** eruption, a huge, glowing, frothy cloud of **tephra** forces its way out of the volcano. The gas, ash, and dust can roll down the side of the volcano as a thick, rumbling mass. These dense, ashy clouds are glowing hot at an amazing temperature of 1048°F (600°C). This phenomenon is known as a **nuée ardente** —French for "blazing cloud." It can move down a slope at 60 miles (100 kilometers) per hour and can stretch for up to 6 miles (10 kilometers). Nuée ardentes are hotter and more dense than most other types of **pyroclastic flow,** and they are extremely dangerous.

Some volcanoes rise so high that ice and snow settle on their summits. When these volcanoes explode, ash mixes with the snow and ice, turning it into a mudslide known as a **lahar.** Lahars are fast-flowing and can smother everything in their way, like this village in the Philippines.

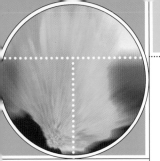

Affecting the Weather

Violent volcanic eruptions are often followed by fantastic sunsets. The sun's rays are bent and split by the gases and ash thrown up high into the sky. It has long been believed that volcanic eruptions of gas and ash also affect the weather. Millions of years ago, they may have caused the formation of the world's climates by creating our atmosphere.

Plinian eruptions can hurl masses of gas and ash high up into the air, right up through the **troposphere** and into the **stratosphere.** In the troposphere the ash can screen the sun for several days, or even weeks, often spreading for hundreds of miles from the volcano itself. The gases can mix with water vapor in clouds and form acid rain. They can also reach 30 miles (50 kilometers) into the stratosphere, where the fine dust can stay for several years. The tiny particles are kept aloft by turbulent air and can drift all the way around the earth, filtering out the light from the sun and lowering temperatures —sometimes by as much as 1.8° F (1° C).

Dust, ash, and gas particles can cause lightning storms that are dangerous to aircraft. Worse, the particles can clog engines. During the month after the Plinian eruption of Mount Pinatubo in the Philippines in June 1991, nine jet aircraft were forced to make emergency landings because of ash-damaged engines.

These long, sloping plains in eastern Oregon are made up of layers of solidified flood **basalt**. They were formed by **hotspot** eruptions between 15.5 and 17.5 million years ago. By examining fossils in the coal-like bottom layer, we have learned that the area once had a warm climate, with large walnut trees, spruces, and Douglas firs. In the upper layers, none of these tree fossils exist, suggesting that the eruptions may have cooled the climate.

Volcano notes

- On the island of Sumbawa in Indonesia, from April 10-12, 1815, there was a massive Plinian eruption of Mount Tambora. For two days the nearby islands were plunged into darkness. The following year, the world had no summer. In New England during the summer, temperatures dropped below the freezing point at night. Crops were ruined by frost.

- After the eruption of Mount Pinatubo in the Philippines on June 15, 1991, an estimated 20 million tons of sulfuric acid, ash, and water vapor exploded into the atmosphere. Satellites tracked these particles and found that by July 11 they had reached far into northern Europe and southern America. By July 15, some had been scattered around the world. The year 1992 was cooler than normal.

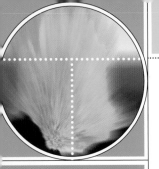

Rumbling Earth, Raging Waves

Volcanic activity is often closely linked with earthquakes. Volcanoes and earthquakes cause one of nature's most powerful and frightening natural disasters—the **tsunami.**

Walls of water

A tsunami is a parade of fast-moving waves that grow higher as the ocean gets shallower near the shore. They are often called tidal waves, but this is misleading —they have nothing to do with tides.

Tsunamis occur when a large mass of water is moved rapidly, usually by earthquakes but sometimes by volcanic activity. This can happen deep on the ocean floor or close to the shore. The swell of water makes waves on the surface. These fast, powerful waves can travel across an ocean and become very tall before crashing on a distant shore.

It seems unbelievable, but when water is moved on one side of the massive Pacific Ocean, it can cause a huge tsunami thousands of miles away on the other side. Damage to the shoreline depends on the depth of the water and the width of the bay. Wide, open, deep shorelines usually suffer little from tsunamis. On the other hand, curved, shallow bays concentrate the strength of the tsunami, squeezing more water into a small space. This boosts the height of the waves and their effect on the land. These tsunamis are killers. Boats are battered into splinters, people are completely swept away or dragged under the wave, buildings are crushed, trees are snapped in half or uprooted, and debris is carried far and wide by the wall of water rushing inland.

Volcano notes

Volcanoes can displace water, causing tsunamis, by:

- a violent volcanic eruption under water
- **pyroclastic flows** that run into the sea
- landslides into the sea following a volcanic eruption on land, or around the seabed after an underwater explosion.

On August 26, 1883, on the island of Krakatau, a massive volcano exploded with such force that for 60 hours a cloak of ash turned day into night. Over 30 miles (50 kilometers) away, on the island of Java, waves reaching 130 feet (40 meters) high swamped the coastline, killing 60,000 people. Krakatau, shown here, is still an active volcano.

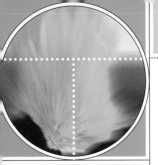

Taking the Pulse

No one knows exactly what a volcano will do next, especially if it has been **dormant** for a very long time, but **vulcanologists** have developed many ways of measuring the slight changes in an active volcano just before it erupts. Some monitoring can take place on volcanoes through "windows." These are holes in the solidified **lava** right near the **crater.** Lava speed, temperature, and gas readings can be taken through these windows. A measurement of the rate at which gas escapes can be taken at the **fumaroles** on the sides of volcanoes.

Volcano notes

These are some of the different ways scientists can monitor volcanic activity to try and predict an eruption.

- Making **microgravity** measurements to pick up any changes in the amount of **magma** below a volcano.
- Measuring weakening electrical signals that occur in the rock as a volcano is about to erupt.
- Measuring the pressure changes inside the volcano as the movement of magma increases.
- Detecting tilting of the earth's surface due to the movement of magma, using tiltmeters.
- Taking **seismic** readings—vibrations increase as the volcano is about to erupt.
- Measuring gas emissions that become more acidic when an eruption is about to take place.
- Measuring higher levels of sulfur dioxide, hydrochloric acid, and hydrogen fluoride, which are often found in gas emissions just before an eruption.
- Reading the temperature of lava, using a pyrometer—it often increases shortly before an eruption.
- Using radar to track the speed of lava flow, which usually increases when a volcano is about to erupt.

The methods listed in the box all hold dangers for the vulcanologists who install the equipment and take the readings. A new monitoring system, called COSTEC, can be used about 30 miles (50 kilometers) from the volcano. The equipment detects concentrations of sulfur dioxide rising into the air by measuring the amount and strength of sunlight shining through it.

Hot news

The very latest development in volcano prediction is being worked on by a scientist named Milton Garces. From the surface of the crater he measures changes in **infrasound,** wavelengths of sound that the human ear cannot detect. These vibrate right from the **magma chamber,** up through the **conduit** and into the **vent.**

This is a volcano observatory at Sakurajima in Japan. Tunnels have been drilled 600 feet (182 meters) into the volcano and a sealed chamber holds equipment to measure changes in pressure, tilt, and vibration. These can be analyzed instantly and, if they are thought to be dangerous, the local authorities and the public will immediately be alerted.

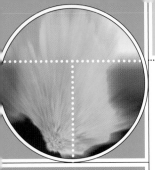

Watching Water

Assessing steam

Searing hot water vapor is a major component of **Plinian** eruptions, and also of the more gentle **fumaroles** and **geysers.** The temperature and sulfur content of vapor from fumaroles rises before an eruption, so monitoring them can be a useful volcano prediction tool. It does not work all the time, but it certainly gave a life-saving warning in Iceland in 1961, before the Askja eruption.

Geysers can also help predict earthquakes. Some geysers, such as Old Faithful at Yellowstone Park, erupt at very regular intervals. If their pattern changes, it is an early sign that the ground underneath is moving, and that magma may be moving closer to the surface. Earth tremors and volcanic activity can also cause **tsunamis.** How are these predicted?

How can you stop a tsunami? It isn't easy, but Japan has led the way by building breakwaters— barriers that break up the waves as they hit the shore —and series of concrete walls to protect coastal communities.

Setting up systems

Hawaii is a **hotspot**—it lies where earthquakes rumble and volcanoes fume. These movements can cause tsunamis elsewhere in the Pacific Ocean, but Hawaii is also affected by tremors and eruptions from other parts of the ocean. This is why, in 1946, the National Oceanographic and Atmospheric Administration (NOAA) chose to set up a warning system in Hawaii now known as the Pacific Tsunami Warning System (PTWS). **Seismic** and tide stations monitor the Pacific Basin from all the main harbors in the region. Large tremors will set off a tsunami watch, and even a small rise in the normal level of seawater will trigger an automatic response.

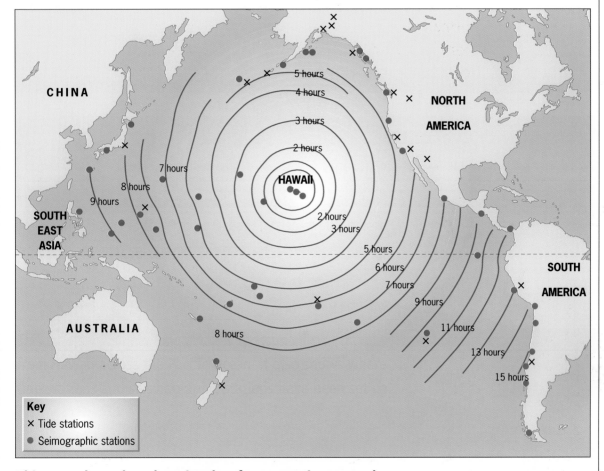

Key
× Tide stations
● Seimographic stations

This map shows how long it takes for tsunamis to travel from Hawaii across the Pacific Ocean. It also shows where tide stations and seismographic stations have been set up.

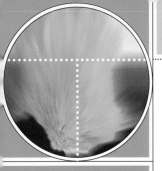

Preventing the Damage

The only way to prevent disaster is to keep people from living near volcanoes, but in our crowded world this is impossible. Good monitoring systems and early evacuation, then, are the only practical ways to reduce the number of deaths. We can also build barriers around **craters** to redirect **lava** and **lahar** flows, and pipe water from crater lakes so that eruptions do not turn into lahars.

Volcano notes

The Japanese government has taken some measures to protect the people of the city of Sakurajima.

- Concrete channels and dams have been built to divert lahars.

- An observatory has been built.

- Concrete shelters have been built along the roadsides.

- Emergency **evacuation** practice takes place every year.

- Education informs people about the risks of eruptions.

Vestmannaeyjar is an important fishing port off the coast of Iceland. In 1973 a lava flow threatened to run into the sea, closing off the harbor. For ten months firefighters and fishermen attacked the lava with jets of water pumped from the sea.

Rich and poor

Why did 2,000 people die in the 1982 eruption of El Chichon in Mexico? And why were 25,000 killed by a lahar in Nevado del Ruiz, Colombia, in 1985? The technology to monitor these volcanoes existed. People could have been evacuated, but they died because their governments could not afford to buy the equipment to set up monitoring stations or emergency shelters. Many such countries spend a lot of their income paying back loans to rich nations. But after Nevado del Ruiz, Colombia built the best volcano observatory in the whole of South America.

In 1992, Mount Etna in Italy erupted, and the village of Zafferana Etnea stood in the way. A dam was built and lava channels were blasted so that the flow changed direction. Giant wire mesh and concrete plugs were also dropped into the lava to stop its flow.

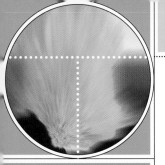

Victims of Volcanoes

Monitoring equipment and modern warning systems have helped to prevent death through volcanic eruptions. However, in the last 100 years, the average number of people killed every year has actually increased. This is because the world's population has boomed, and many people have been forced to live close to volcano hazard areas in order to make a living. So while many people have been saved through modern technology and early **evacuation,** many have also died.

Homeless

As we have seen, the people of Monserrat in the Caribbean once lived on a flourishing, fertile island. But they also lived in the shadow of volcanoes that, in 1995, began to belch out tons of ash and **lava.** Life in the south of the island came to a standstill, crops were destroyed, and towns were buried under tons of heavy, clogging ash. Any place where people live on the slopes of an active volcano, they run the risk of losing their homes to lava flows, clouds of blanketing ash, and mudslides.

The huge ash clouds descending from the Soufriere Hills on the island of Monserrat forced people from their homes in 1997.

Killing crops

Thick carpets of ash covering crops and pastures were once a huge problem in disaster zones, causing starvation and mass migration. People are now evacuated to other areas, they are given new land to farm, and herds of animals are replaced. Although there is still hardship, it is now less likely that famine will follow eruptions.

Immediately after a disaster, governments and aid agencies are able to assess needs very rapidly. They act quickly to bring emergency food rations and clean water into the disaster area. Modern communication networks and better road, rail, and air facilities have made this fast response possible. Nevertheless, poorer parts of the world are still going to suffer more than richer ones. In poorer countries, too, many more people have to live close to danger.

In Iceland in 1783, over 9,000 people starved to death after an eruption burst through a deep crack in Mount Laki, pictured here. Massive emissions of gas poisoned the grasslands and crops. Half the cattle in Iceland died, as did more than three-quarters of the sheep—the main sources of meat and clothing in this sparse countryside.

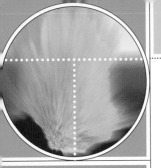

Why Live in Danger?

About ten percent of the world's population lives close to active volcanoes. Even though only about three percent of all eruptions endanger lives and property, there are still about 500 million people living in danger. The biggest problem is not being able to predict exactly when, where, and with what force volcanoes will erupt. This insecurity has not prevented people from living with the threat—so why do they do it?

Farming in the shadows

There are a few advantages to living near volcanoes. Farmers are attracted to volcanic slopes by the rich, well-drained soils. Some of these soils are **lahars** that have been broken down by the wind and rain. They are full of **nitrogen,** which help crops to grow.

On certain volcanic islands, such as the Philippines, the population is increasing so fast that farmland is becoming scarce. This has forced people to plant crops on the slopes of Mayon, an active volcano. The richness of the soil enables a wide range of plants to be grown, from rice and vegetables to coconut palms. But the risks became clear in 1993, when 75 tomato farmers were killed in an eruption.

Building blocks

Volcanoes provide good, instant building materials, too. For example, ash can be used to make cement. Hardened **lava** and **tuff rings,** where exploded volcanic rocks around the edge of a **maar** or **crater** have become compacted into a light but solid rock wall, are cut into building blocks. In Italy and Turkey, cave houses, shops, and animal shelters have actually been carved into steep tuff rocks, which keep out both the winter cold and the summer heat.

The land where this volcano in Paricutin, Mexico, now sits was once a cornfield. On February 20, 1943, a great crack opened in the ground and by the next day, a **cinder cone** 30 feet (10 meters) high rose above the fields, with hot rocks spitting from its center. It stopped erupting nine years later, and now sits about 1,400 feet (424 meters) above ground, with thick ash spread all around.

Mount Rainier is a breathtaking volcano, only 30 miles (50 kilometers) away from Seattle. **Vulcanologists** fear that in the event of an eruption, millions of people in this area are at risk from mudflows that could sweep down the river valleys.

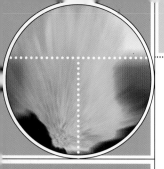

Hot Water

We have seen that sprays of extremely hot water and steam can explode out of a volcano, putting people in danger. Not all volcanically heated water is dangerous, however. Some of it is a very useful natural energy resource—one more reason for living on the edge.

Hot water and central heating

Bubbling hot springs, gushing **geysers,** the fine sprays of **fumaroles,** and boiling mud pools are spectacular sights. They attract both scientists and tourists. In addition, they can be a valuable source of heat energy.

These steaming features form when hot **magma** and volcanic rock heat the groundwater above them, which then expands and rises to the surface as hot water or steam. For hundreds of years people have visited these springs, which are thought to have healing power.

All the world's energy needs could easily be met by tapping into the hot **mantle** that wraps itself around the earth—if only we could get to it! In most places, it lies 30 miles (50 kilometers) below the earth's surface and is too difficult to reach. However, we can still use natural sources of hot water and steam near volcanic centers.

For nearly 100 years, geysers in Italy have been used to generate electric power. The rising steam is strong enough to turn **steam turbines** that then generate electricity. Since then, countries such as Iceland and New Zealand, as well as the state of California, have developed heating systems and generators from active, volcanically-heated water. This power source is known as **geothermal energy.** The buildings in Iceland's capital city, Rejkyavik, are all heated using geothermal energy.

Drilling deep

Nowadays, engineers not only tap into natural geysers, they also drill boreholes close to the raised magma source. There is always the chance that an eruption will send everything sky-high. Engineers are also experimenting with hardened, hot rocks near volcanic centers that have been inactive for millions of years. In Cornwall, England, and in Los Alamos, New Mexico, they are trying to drill down to this kind of hot rock. Then water can be pumped onto it, creating steam that can be used to generate geothermal energy. The steam can even be recycled—first it is cooled and **condensed** into water droplets, then it can be pumped down into the borehole again.

As the water around a hot spring cools, valuable **minerals** form a crust of multicolored crystals around the hot-water holes—bright yellow, blue, pink, and green.

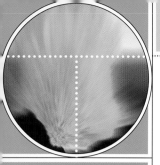

Life on Earth

Volcanoes take life, but they make life, too. Four billion years ago they started to shape our earth, building continents and giving out the water and gases that make life on it possible. Then out of this steamy chaos grew microorganisms, plants, animals—and humans.

Krakatau—a natural disaster

Krakatau, a tropical island in Indonesia, was blasted into pieces on August 26, 1883. Its once lush forest, teeming with brightly-colored birds and insects, was smothered in ash or swamped by the sea. Three volcanoes exploded, one after another, in four huge eruptions of **pumice,** gas, and ash. The island collapsed in a series of debris avalanches. In the north, two of the volcanoes, Perbuwata and Danan, completely vanished under the waves. In the south, the island was split into two, half of its **caldera** sliding into the sea. Almost no living thing was spared, and darkness fell over the island for two days as ash and gas filled the skies.

The island was empty, but for how long? Just 100 years later, Krakatau—now called Pulau Rakata—was once more teeming with life. The island has provided scientists with an opportunity to find out how long it takes for a volcanic island to recover from an eruption. How did this gray, isolated island become green again?

Rakata has a tropical climate—over 79 inches (2000 millimeters) of rain fall each year, and the temperature is warm. These conditions broke down the pumice and ash into fertile soil, leaving it ready and waiting for any plant life that made its way across the sea. About 9 miles (15 kilometers) of water lie between Rakata and the large island of Sumatra, and about 16 miles (25 kilometers) between Rakata and Java. Seeds, birds, reptiles, amphibians, and mammals found their way from these two islands to the volcanic wilderness.

Just one year after the eruptions, a scientist found a wind-blown spider crawling across the rocks. Large seedpods from the tall needle and pandanas trees floated across the water, were washed ashore, and rooted into the ash. Windblown fern and moss spores and flower seeds landed on the island, flourishing under the shade of the growing forest. Snakes swam across the straits. Geckoes floated on scraps of wood and land spiders on swarms of plankton—the tiniest sea plants on earth. Birds such as bee-eaters, woodpeckers, and the Philippine glossy starling found new homes among the empty trees. Mongooses and rats swam ashore, hoping to feed on their eggs. The relationships between natural things had begun to take shape. The sea itself became a rich haven for fish, such as the large tuna. Fish-loving sea birds, like the large frigate, followed the shoals. Life had returned to Krakatau.

Volcanic activity does not necessarily destroy natural life for long. Ganung Api in Indonesia is an active volcano, but it supports a vast quantity of natural plant and animal life on its slopes.

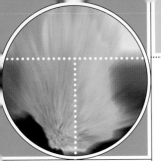

Volcanoes in History

Evidence of the most ancient volcanoes can be seen in the shapes they made on the world's landscape and the rocks and precious stones they hurled from the earth's core. We can also tell the timing of volcanic activity hundreds of thousands of years ago by studying remnants of plant life that were caught up in **basaltic lava** flows. Ice samples, called **ice cores,** drilled out at the poles reveal greater levels of acid when eruptions occurred. Tree rings show poor growth during the cool years that often follow a massive eruption. But how do we know what happened to people struck by a volcanic disaster in ancient times?

The Italian volcano Mount Etna (meaning "I burn") is the oldest continually erupting volcano in Europe. It has oozed and burst 100 times in the last 4,000 years, and written records of its eruptions date back over 2,000 years.

The Plinys of Pompeii

A young writer named Pliny described the eruptions of Vesuvius, on the Bay of Naples, in A.D. 79—nearly 2,000 years ago. It followed a devastating earthquake in A.D. 62, which had toppled part of Pompeii, a city of 20,000 people lying in the shadows of Vesuvius. Seventeen years later, the rebuilding was still in progress when, on August 24, A.D. 79, massive **Plinian** eruptions exploded, releasing 1 cubic mile (4.13 cubic kilometers) of ash, **pumice,** and toxic gas.

Down the mountain it roared—over Pompeii, its surrounding towns and villages, and into the sea. Pliny described the progress of the eruptions, from an innocent-looking mushroom-shaped cloud to the **pyroclastic flows** that killed 2000 people. Among the dead were young Pliny's uncle, also named Pliny, who was a famous Roman scientist and commander of the navy. He may have been **suffocated** by the sulfur fumes, or possibly he died from shock. Others were swamped in burning ash, suffocated by hot gas, or killed by falling pillars and bricks. We know about their suffering not only because of young Pliny's descriptions, but also because their bodies were well preserved by the volcanic ash. This is the scene Pliny witnessed when the worst was over:

> *"After a while, the darkness paled into smoke or cloud, and the real daylight returned but the sun was still shining as wanly as during an eclipse. We were amazed by what we saw because everything had changed and was buried deep in ash like snow."*

Pliny the Younger's writings are studied by both historians and **vulcanologists.** His uncle, Pliny the Elder, gave his name to the most devastating eruption there is—Plinian.

Many volcanoes have become sacred to the people living in their shadow. The Ancient Greeks and Romans believed that the active island of Vulcano was the home of the god of fire, and this is where we get the word "volcano." Mount Fuji, shown here, is considered to be sacred by the Japanese. No one knows if it is truly **extinct.**

Amazing Volcanoes

Volcanoes are deadly, but they are amazing and fascinating, too. Here are some fantastic facts about volcanoes.

The ten most deadly

Not all these deaths listed here were caused directly by volcanoes. Some were the result of **tsunamis** and later starvation due to crops being destroyed.

Volcano	Place	Year	Number of deaths
Tambora	Jambawa, Indonesia	1815	92,000
Krakatau	Krakatau, Indonesia	1883	36,500
Mont Pelée	Martinique, West Indies	1902	29,000
Nevado del Ruiz	Armero, Colombia	1985	25,000
Mount Etna	Sicily, Italy	1669	20,000
Mount Vesuvius	Bay of Naples, Italy	79	20,000
Kelut	Java, Indonesia	1586	10,000
Laki	Iceland	1783	9,500
Santa Maria	Guatemala, Central America	1902	6,000
Kelut	Java, Indonesia	1919	5,000

The next big one

Where and when will the next big eruption occur? Scientists are most worried about those **dormant** volcanoes that have kept quiet for hundreds of years. When these do erupt, they are usually the most destructive of all. This is because a plug of **magma** has often solidified inside the **conduit,** and the magma and gases underneath it are highly pressurized—and highly explosive.

The East African Rift Valley is a huge split in the African continental **tectonic plate** over 2,500 miles (4,000 kilometers) long. Through it, volcanic activity has bubbled and burst from time to time for millions of years.

Mount Vesuvius in Italy has lain quiet for nearly 2,000 years, smoldering gently from its **crater.** Wedged inside the conduit is a huge blob of solidified magma 197 feet (60 meters) wide. **Vulcanologists** cannot predict when or how an eruption might occur. Two million people live in the danger zone.

What killed the dinosaurs?

Did volcanic eruptions kill off the dinosaurs? There are many theories—a large meteor impact being the most popular—but there is some evidence to suggest that volcanoes could have played their part, too. Between five and ten huge explosions coincided with major **extinctions** of different species of dinosaur. One of these occurred 65 million years ago at the end of the Cretaceous period, when it is believed that the last dinosaurs died out. The eruption occurred in the Deccan Province in India. It is thought that about a thousand megatons of sulfuric acid spurted into the atmosphere, blocking out sunlight and causing acid rain. Plants were killed by the lack of sunlight and the poisonous rain, so the dinosaurs had no food.

45

Glossary

a'a lava   basaltic lava flow with a rough, jagged surface

andesite   fine-grained volcanic rock containing 55-70 percent silica

basalt   fine-grained, dark-colored volcanic rock containing less than 55 percent silica

batholith   large body of magma that lies below the surface. When solidified, it can be eroded into a dome shape.

buoyant   able to float

caldera   huge crater caused by the collapse of a magma chamber

cinder cone   steep-sided volcano with a small crater at the top, made up of small basalt rocks

colonize   to establish a colony—plants, animals, or humans—in a particular area

composite volcano   volcano made up of different layers of ash and lava

condense   to convert from vapor to liquid when cooled

conduit   tunnel that leads from a volcano's magma chamber to the vent

crater   hole in the top of a volcano cone through which it erupts

delta   new land formed by material deposited at the mouth of a river

dome   dome-shaped volcano

dormant   not active, but not completely dead or extinct

dike   magma that forces its way through a vertical crack in layers of rock, making a vertical sheet through them

erode   to wear away by the action of water, wind, and gravity

evacuate   to leave a dangerous area

extinct   no longer active

fumarole   fine hot spray of steam or gas that sprays up from hot volcanic rock under the earth's surface

geological   relating to the physical properties of the earth

geothermal energy   energy created by heat or steam from magma

geothermal vent   opening in the earth through which steam and gases escape

geyser   hot water spout, like a fountain, that spurts up from hot volcanic rock under the earth's surface

granite   hard rock formed by slow cooling of rhyolitic magma underground

gravity   force that attracts objects to each other, depending on their mass

Hawaiian   type of gentle eruption of gas and lava in the form of fountains

hotspot   area of long-term volcanic activity not associated with tectonic plate motion

ice core   sample of ice from an ice cap or sheet showing its yearly layers

Icelandic   calm, oozing type of eruption

infrasound   type of sound wave that vibrates from a volcano's magma chamber and up through the vent

insulated   protected from extreme heat or cold

laccolith   layer of magma that pushes up between other layers of horizontal rock, then forms a dome shape

lahar   river of mud formed when ash mixes with water, snow, or ice

lava   molten rock that oozes or flows above the earth's surface

maar   wide, gently-sloping crater formed from a single explosive eruption

magma   molten rock beneath the earth's surface

magma chamber   well of magma that seeps up into the earth's crust

mantle   layer of hot rock that lies between the earth's crust and core

microgravity   tiny changes in the gravity field over the earth's surface

mineral   chemical substance found in rock or the ground

nitrogen   element that acts as a fertilizer when plants' roots take it in from the soil

nuée ardente   "blazing cloud" of erupted volcanic ash, gas, and other material

pahoehoe lava   basaltic lava flow that hardens into a smooth, gently rolling sheet

percolate   to seep through rock that has tiny holes or cracks in it

phacolith   small wave of magma that pushes between other layers of rock

Plinian   type of eruption that shoots out hot ash and gases high into the air

pumice   frothy, gassy lava that cools into stone with many tiny bubble holes

pyroclastic flow   dense, fast-flowing nuée ardente

rhyolite   volcanic rock containing more than 70 percent silica

sea-floor spreading   process by which new ocean floor is created when plates pull apart and new volcanic material rises up and solidifies

seismic   having to do with the vibration of the earth

seismology   study of earthquakes

shield volcano   volcano shaped like a thick pancake made from basalt lava flows

silica   compound of oxygen and silicon

silicon   common element in rocks

sill   horizontal layer of hardened magma that has forced between layers of rock

steam turbine   motor that is driven by steam, which turns an electric generator

stratosphere   layer of atmosphere just above the troposphere

Strombolian   type of eruption that shoots out fountains of basaltic and andesitic lava and lava bombs

subduction zone   place where one edge of a tectonic plate slips down beneath the edge of another plate

suffocate   to die from lack of oxygen

tectonic plate   huge slab of the earth's crust that moves at a very slow rate

tephra   ash, glass, crystals, and rock fragments ejected from a volcano when it erupts

troposphere   layer of atmosphere closest to the earth

tsunami   high-energy ocean waves caused by volcanic activity or earthquakes

tuff ring   solidified magma forming a raised edge around a maar

vent   opening at the top of a volcano

Vesuvian   type of very violent eruption that explodes through a hard cap in the top of a volcano

viscous   slow-flowing

vulcanologist   scientist who studies volcanoes

More Books to Read

DK Publishing staff. *Volcano.* New York: DK Publishing, 1999.

Martin, Fred. *Volcano.* Chicago: Heinemann Library, 1998.

Meister, Cari. *Volcanoes.* Minneapolis, Minn.: ABDO Publishing Co., 1999.

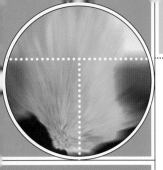

Index